MOMMY, WHAT IS LUPUS?

Written by Nadria Givens
Illustrated by Abdul Mueed

Printed in the United States of America
Mommy, What is Lupus?

ISBN 9798514146611
Ballard Publishing Group, LLC.

My mommy doesn't always feel the best. She has something that's called Systemic Lupus. I wanted to know what exactly lupus was and why it kept making my mommy feel so sick, so I decided to ask her.

Last week when Mom got home from the hospital, I walked over to her, looked up at her and asked, "Mommy, what is Lupus?"

My mom looked down at me and smiled. As I looked at her face, I could tell she was surprised by my question. She took a moment to think before answering me.

"Well, Lupus is a disease. It causes my body to attack itself. It can attack important parts of my body such as my heart and lungs. My body believes it is fighting an infection everyday, but it's really fighting itself." My mom replied.

I was still confused, so my mom asked, "You have no idea what I'm talking about, do you?"

“Close your eyes. Imagine a war going on inside my body. My body is attacking itself because it does not know what is good or bad. My body thinks EVERYTHING is bad like a cold or the flu,” she said.

When I closed my eyes, I imagined a battle going on in my mommy’s body. I could picture her heart being attacked. It made me sad.

"How did you get lupus?" I asked.

Mommy said, "No one really knows what causes Lupus. It's definitely not my fault or yours. You can't catch lupus from someone or give it to someone else, so it isn't contagious."

I asked, “What’s it called when you feel sick?”

“When I feel sick from Lupus, it’s called a flare. Flares can cause my body to ache, I get really tired, and sometimes it is hard for me to breathe.” Mommy sadly replied. “When it gets too bad, I must go to the hospital.”

“I don't like it when you go to go to the hospital. It makes me feel very sad. I don't like to see you feeling so sick. That's the worse feeling in the world.” I said.

She hugged me tightly and said, “There are things that doctors can do to make me feel better that I can’t do at home. And the faster I get better, the sooner I come home to you.”

I whispered, “I don’t want you to have anymore flares.”

"Even though there's no cure yet, there's a lot I can do to try to prevent flares. I can make sure I take my medication. I have to eat nutritious foods, like fruits and vegetables. I also have to exercise and have a positive attitude." Mommy explained.

I looked up at her and smiled.

"I love you mommy. I promise to always help you remember to take your medicine, eat your veggies and go for long walks." I said.

She asked, “Do you understand a little better about lupus?”

“Yes, mommy I do,” I whispered.

www.ingramcontent.com/pod-product-compliance
Ingram Content Group UK Ltd.
Pitfield, Milton Keynes, MK11 3LW, UK
UKHW060116300726
14090UKWH00002B/216

* 9 7 9 8 5 1 4 1 4 6 6 1 1 *